Our Lady of Guadalupe

Retold by
Carmen T.
Bernier-Grand

Illustrated by
Tonya
Engel

Marshall Cavendish Children

One morning a long time ago, Juan Diego got up to go to Mass, just as he did every day. He tiptoed by his elderly uncle so as not to wake him up. In the darkness before dawn, Juan Diego fastened his coarse *tilma* to his left shoulder.

On bare feet he set out to walk the nine miles to Tlatelolco. Mist veiled the road, and the air smelled like incense.

When Juan Diego reached Tepeyac Hill, he heard music. It was so tender, he stopped to listen, but then the music stopped.

A woman called, "Juanito! Juan Dieguito!"

What is a woman doing on top of this barren, rocky hill at dawn? Juan Diego wondered.

He climbed up to see who it was. Blessed day! The nopal cacti were as bright as emeralds. Blessed sight! The young lady at the summit was framed by sun rays that shone from her like blazing flames. The rebozo that covered her head was the color of a blue, starry twilight.

"I am the Virgin Mary, Mother of the true God," she said in Juan Diego's language, Nahuatl.

Am I dreaming? Juan Diego asked himself. *Am I in heaven? How can a poor Aztec like me be worthy of what I am seeing and hearing? What can the Blessed Virgin want from me?*

"I would like a shrine built on this hill," she said. "When you get to Tlatelolco, please visit the bishop. Tell him what you have seen and heard."

"But I am a nobody. I am a small rope, a tiny ladder, the tail end, a leaf," Juan Diego replied. "Why would the bishop listen to me?"

"Am I not here, your Mother?" said the Virgin. "Are you not under my shadow and protection? Am I not the fountain of your joy?"

Juan Diego nodded. "I, your humble servant, will talk to the bishop."

He scrambled down the hill and hurried to reach the bishop's palace.

"Please announce me," Juan Diego told the servants. "I have a message for the bishop."

"An Indian wants an audience with the bishop?" The servants laughed.

Juan Diego stood outside the palace, waiting to be called. Other people who had arrived after him were ushered in. Juan Diego, who had had no breakfast, grew hungry. Three hours passed. Would he be able to deliver the message?

After everyone else had been escorted inside, finally he was called.

Juan Diego bowed before the bishop. He told him what he had heard and seen.

"If you see her again, return, my son," the bishop said. Then he dismissed the poor Indian.

What made me think that a bishop would take an Aztec seriously? Juan Diego asked himself as he scurried back to Tepeyac Hill. *I need to tell the Virgin what happened, but maybe she won't appear to me again. Maybe I was dreaming when I saw her.*

Juan Diego climbed to the top of the hill.

It was not a dream! There she was!

"The bishop thinks I am making this up," he said. "Please, My Lady, send somebody important to deliver your message."

"Listen, my son," the Virgin replied. "There are many I could send, but you are the one I have chosen. Tomorrow you must return to the bishop. Tell him it is the ever-holy Virgin Mary who sends you, and repeat to him my great desire for a shrine on this hill."

On Sunday morning, Juan Diego again walked the nine miles to the bishop's palace.

"I have a message from Our Lady," Juan Diego told the servants.

Again the servants laughed. Again Juan Diego had to wait until the bishop had seen everyone else. Again it was hours before he was called in.

"Once more I have seen the ever-holy Virgin Mary," Juan Diego told the bishop.

"What does she look like?" the bishop asked.

"Her skin glows, as if she has a touch of all bloods. The stars in her blue rebozo look like the constellations of the night sky. The back of her left hand has a painted *yollo*, a heart but with flames above. She also wears a black sash as pregnant women do. Her feet stand firmly on a crescent moon. The volcanoes on her gown are embroidered with gold thread. But she bows her head. That tells me that she is not an Aztec goddess. There is a higher power above her."

"I don't know if you are lying or dreaming," the bishop said.

Tears poured down Juan Diego's face. "I was as awake when I saw her as I am now. I am telling the truth. Please, make the Virgin's wish come true."

The bishop shook
his head. "I need
a sign if I am to
believe."
Juan Diego
bowed. "I will ask
the Lady for a sign."
He left right away.

"My Lady," he said at the top of Tepeyac Hill. "The bishop asked for a sign that will prove that I have seen you."

"Well and good. I will give you a sign. Come back tomorrow, and your wish will be granted."

"Thank you, My Lady. I want to be believed."

When Juan Diego got home, he found his uncle sick with *cocolixtl*, a high fever that normally led to death. On Monday, Juan Diego knew the Virgin was waiting for him, but he couldn't leave his uncle alone.

On Tuesday, his uncle had grown much weaker. "Please, bring in a priest to hear my last confession," he told Juan Diego.

Juan Diego fastened his *tilma* and in haste walked toward Tlatelolco. As he got near Tepeyac Hill, he thought, *The Virgin will be angry that I didn't visit her yesterday. I will go to the left so she will not see me.*

"My son, what is the matter?" Juan Diego heard behind him. He turned and fell to his knees. The Virgin stood at the foot of the hill.

"I . . . ," Juan Diego said. "I wanted to come yesterday, but my uncle is dying. He needs a priest."

"Do not be distressed or afraid," she said. "Your uncle will not die now. Go up to the top of the hill. Cut the flowers growing there and bring them to me."

"Flowers in December?"

"Yes, my son."

Juan Diego climbed the hill, thinking he would find nothing but cactus flowers. Instead, he found Castilian roses that grew only in Spain!

He plucked an armful, looped up his *tilma*, and carried the roses down. The Virgin Mary rearranged the roses cradled in the *tilma*. She tied both bottom corners of the cactus cloak to his neck and instructed him to show the roses to the bishop.

Juan Diego walked to the bishop's palace, holding his looped *tilma*, careful not to drop the roses, and smelling their sweet scent.

The bishop's servants smelled them, too. "What do you have in your *tilma*?" they asked.

"Roses," Juan Diego answered.

The servants laughed. "Roses in December?"

"Yes."

"Go on in," one said. "Go on in and tell the bishop."

When Juan Diego got inside, he bowed before the bishop and untied the *tilma*. The roses dropped to the floor like a flock of red birds flying to the ground. The bishop sprang from his chair, fell to his knees, and crossed himself. The awestruck servants did the same.

The image of the Blessed
Virgin Mary was painted on
Juan Diego's *tilma*!

"Thank you, My Lady," Juan
Diego said.

"My son," the bishop told
him, "I will build the shrine."

When Juan Diego got home, his uncle had risen in his bed. "A luminous young woman stood right here and told me I would get well. She said to call her Our Lady of Guadalupe."

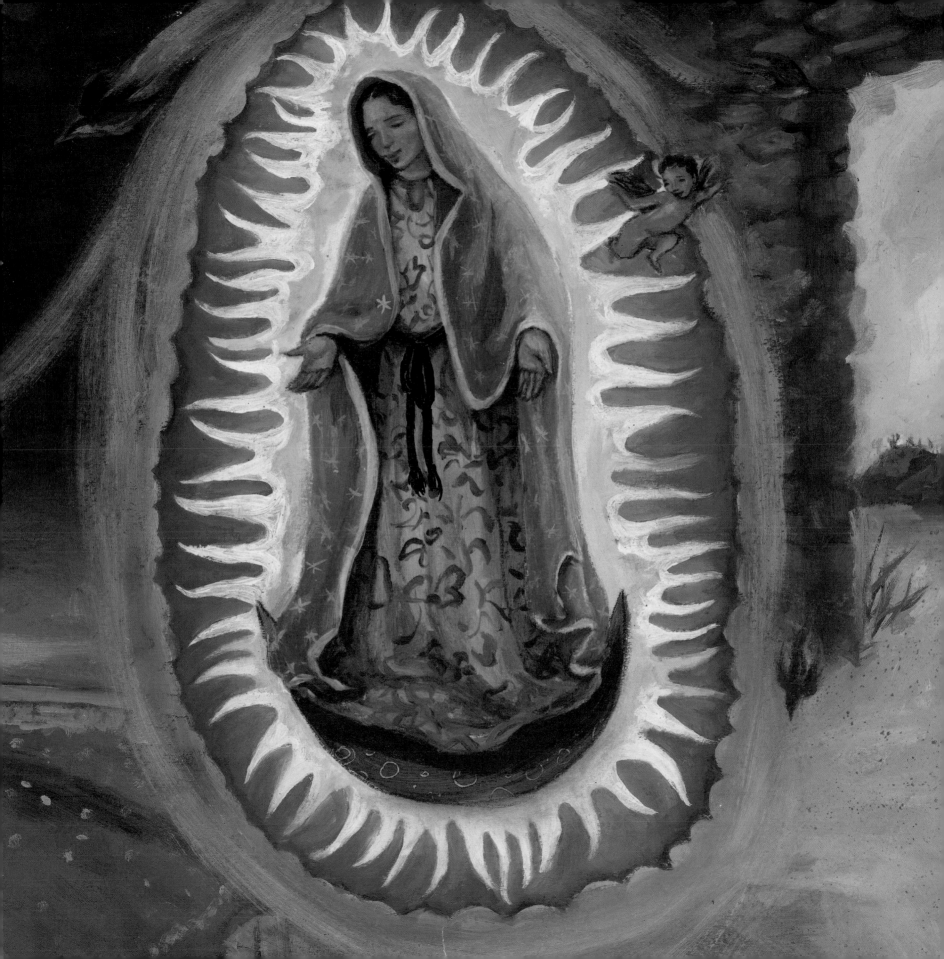

Juan Diego didn't see the Virgin again. But two years later, he became the guardian of the shrine that the bishop built on top of Tepeyac Hill.

Today millions of pilgrims visit the sanctuary to pray before the image of Our Lady of Guadalupe on the coarse *tilma* of the humble Aztec, Juan Diego.

In pre-Hispanic times, the Aztecs built a stone temple on Tepeyac Hill dedicated to the earth and fertility goddess Tonantzin, the mother god. Tonantzin was depicted with a head full of snakes, and serpents decorated her garment. Her temple was later destroyed by the Spanish conquistadores, who wanted to convert the Indians to Christianity. It was on that same hill that, according to Juan Diego, Our Lady of Guadalupe appeared to him.

Juan Diego was born in 1467 in Cuautitlán, fourteen miles north of Tlatelolco, now Mexico City. His Aztec name was Cuauhtlatoatzin. Before the Spanish conquest that began in Mexico in 1519, he no doubt worshiped the Aztec goddess Tonantzin.

Between 1524 and 1525, he and his wife converted to Catholicism. She was christened as María Lucía, he as Juan Diego. After María Lucía died in 1529, Juan Diego moved with his Catholic uncle Juan Bernardino to Tolpetlac, nine miles from Tlatelolco.

Juan Diego was fifty-seven years old when, in 1531, he reported the three apparitions (December 9, December 10, and December 12, 1531) of the Virgin Mary on Tepeyac Hill. He said that the Virgin wore a black sash around her waist, meaning she was with child (Tonantzin was the goddess of fertility), and that the Virgin told him she was the Mother of the True God (Tonantzin was the mother god). But unlike the Aztec goddess, the Virgin Mary bowed her head.

After a fourth apparition (also on December 12, 1531), Juan Diego's uncle told Juan Diego that Our Lady had said her name was Coatlaxopeuh, pronounced "QWAT-lah-SOO-peh," which sounds like "Guadalupe" in Spanish. Consequently, the Madonna that Juan Diego said appeared to him was named Our Lady of Guadalupe. But the *coa* in Coatlaxopeuh means "serpent"; *tla* can be interpreted as "the"; and *xopeuh* means "to crush." The Madonna was calling herself "She who crushes the serpent."

When in 1531 the news of the apparitions of Our Lady of Guadalupe spread, some Mexicans thought she was Tonantzin. Many other Mexicans interpreted the name and miracle as signs that their Aztec beliefs had to be replaced with Christianity. When they visited the shrine built by Bishop Juan de Zumárraga, Juan Diego showed them the *tilma* and convincingly described the apparitions. Indians converted to Catholicism by the thousands.

Because the *tilma* was made from the fibers of the maguey cactus, some Mexican artists, such as Miguel Cabrera (1695–1768), said that it was impossible for it to support any form of painting. The *tilma* was expected to deteriorate in roughly thirty years. Yet, after more than 475 years, pilgrims can see a radiant image of Our Lady of Guadalupe from any point within the circular basilica on Tepeyac Hill that today houses the *tilma*.

Photographers, physicians, and ophthalmologists who have had the opportunity to inspect the *tilma* have said that they see human figures reflected in both eyes of the Madonna. In 1979 José Aste Tonsmann, who has a PhD from Cornell University, scanned a photograph of the face of the Virgin on the *tilma* at very high resolution. He reported that the eyes reflect the moment in which Juan Diego showed the bishop the image of the Virgin of Guadalupe.

Every year, more than 7 million people visit the Basilica of Our Lady of Guadalupe, near Mexico City, especially on December 12, the day the miracle happened. She is a central figure in Mexican culture.

On January 23, 1999, Pope John Paul II, referring to the three Americas as one continent, called Our Lady of Guadalupe the Mother of America.

Juan Diego died on May 30, 1548, at the age of seventy-four and was buried on Tepeyac Hill.

On July 31, 2002, Pope John Paul II canonized him a saint.

To my nieces: Daisy Immaculada Bernier, Lisette Marie Campos,
and Margriet Lisette Bernier

—C.T.B-G.

To Taylor Ryan, the love of my life, and to both our families.
I couldn't have taken the journey without the love and dedication of you all!

—T.E.

Text copyright © 2012 by Carmen T. Bernier-Grand
Illustrations copyright © 2012 by Tonya Engel

Marshall Cavendish Corporation, 99 White Plains Road, Tarrytown, NY 10591
www.marshallcavendish.us/kids

Library of Congress Cataloging-in-Publication Data

Bernier-Grand, Carmen T.
Our Lady of Guadalupe / retold by Carmen T. Bernier-Grand ; illustrated by
Tonya Engel. — 1st ed.
p. cm.
ISBN 978-0-7614-6135-7 (hardcover) — ISBN 978-0-7614-6137-1 (ebook)
1. Guadalupe, Our Lady of–Juvenile literature. 2. Juan Diego, Saint,
1474-1548–Juvenile literature. I. Engel, Tonya, ill. II. Title.
BT660.G8B525 2012
232.91'7097253–dc23
2011016398

The illustrations are rendered in oil and encaustics.
Book design by Anahid Hamparian
Editor: Margery Cuyler

Printed in Malaysia (T)
First edition
1 3 5 6 4 2

mc Marshall Cavendish
Children